P9-CQP-946

# Dear Parents:

Congratulations! Your child is taking the first steps on an exciting journey. The destination? Independent reading!

**STEP INTO READING®** will help your child get there. The program offers five steps to reading success. Each step includes fun stories and colorful art or photographs. In addition to original fiction and books with favorite characters, there are Step into Reading Non-Fiction Readers, Phonics Readers and Boxed Sets, Sticker Readers, and Comic Readers—a complete literacy program with something to interest every child.

## Learning to Read, Step by Step!

**Ready to Read   Preschool–Kindergarten**
• big type and easy words • rhyme and rhythm • picture clues
For children who know the alphabet and are eager to begin reading.

**Reading with Help   Preschool–Grade 1**
• basic vocabulary • short sentences • simple stories
For children who recognize familiar words and sound out new words with help.

**Reading on Your Own   Grades 1–3**
• engaging characters • easy-to-follow plots • popular topics
For children who are ready to read on their own.

**Reading Paragraphs   Grades 2–3**
• challenging vocabulary • short paragraphs • exciting stories
For newly independent readers who read simple sentences with confidence.

**Ready for Chapters   Grades 2–4**
• chapters • longer paragraphs • full-color art
For children who want to take the plunge into chapter books but still like colorful pictures.

**STEP INTO READING®** is designed to give every child a successful reading experience. The grade levels are only guides; children will progress through the steps at their own speed, developing confidence in their reading.

Remember, a lifetime love of reading starts with a single step!

© 2018 Spin Master PAW Productions Inc. All rights reserved. Published in the United States by Random House Children's Books, a division of Penguin Random House LLC, 1745 Broadway, New York, NY 10019, and in Canada by Penguin Random House Canada Limited, Toronto. PAW Patrol and all related titles, logos, and characters are trademarks of Spin Master Ltd. Nickelodeon, Nick Jr., and all related titles and logos are trademarks of Viacom International Inc.

Step into Reading, Random House, and the Random House colophon are registered trademarks of Penguin Random House LLC.

Visit us on the Web!
StepIntoReading.com
rhcbooks.com

Educators and librarians, for a variety of teaching tools, visit us at RHTeachersLibrarians.com

ISBN 978-1-5247-7279-6 (trade) — ISBN 978-1-5247-7280-2 (lib. bdg.)

Printed in the United States of America

10 9 8 7 6 5 4 3

Random House Children's Books supports the First Amendment and celebrates the right to read.

2 STEP INTO READING®

STEP
READING WITH HELP

nickelodeon

PAW PATROL

# Up in the AIR!

by Mary Tillworth

based on the teleplay "Pups Save a Plane"
by Charles Johnston

illustrated by Harry Moore

Random House 🏠 New York

Ryder and the pups
are camping in the forest.
They hear a sound
in the sky.

Ace the pilot,
Mayor Goodway,
and Chickaletta
soar by in a plane!

# Ace is teaching
# the mayor how to fly.

The mayor swerves
around a flock of birds.
A wing on the plane breaks!

Ace must fix
the wing!
The mayor steers
the plane.

Ace's sleeve gets caught on the broken wing!

Ace and the mayor
need help!
They call
the PAW Patrol.

Ryder takes the call.
He tells the pups to get
to the Air Patroller!

The Air Patroller
takes off.
The PAW Patrol zooms
to the rescue!

Meanwhile, Ace's plane shakes in the wind. Chickaletta bounces out onto the wing!

The Air Patroller
hovers over Ace's plane.
Skye and Rocky
fly down.

Skye flies Ace's plane.

She is a great pilot.

Rocky uses scissors.

*Snip! Snip!*

He cuts Ace's sleeve.

He frees Ace!

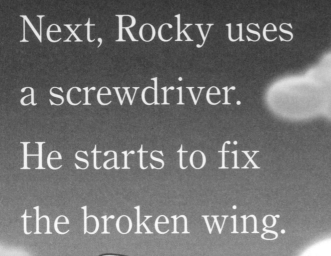

Next, Rocky uses
a screwdriver.
He starts to fix
the broken wing.

Ace tries to save Chickaletta.
She reaches for Chickaletta,
but the chicken
falls off the wing!

Marshall dives
from the Air Patroller.
He soars through
a flock of birds.

# Marshall catches
# Chickaletta on his head!

Marshall returns
Chickaletta to the mayor.
Rocky finishes
fixing the plane wing.

The PAW Patrol saved Ace, the mayor, and Chickaletta! They all roast marshmallows to celebrate.

Hooray for the Sea Patrol!

And hooray for Rocky!

Now he likes to get wet.

Ryder and Zuma
lead the baby octopus
to its mother!
The family is
together again!

Ryder and Zuma
steer the ship
into the ocean.
They shake the rattle.
The baby octopus
follows them.

Rocky wants to help.

He dives into the sea.

He is getting wet!

He finds the rattle

with his metal detector.

Marshall waves the rattle.
The baby octopus
reaches for it.
But the mayor
knocks the rattle
into the sea!

The Sea Patrol
needs to get
the baby octopus
back to its mama fast!

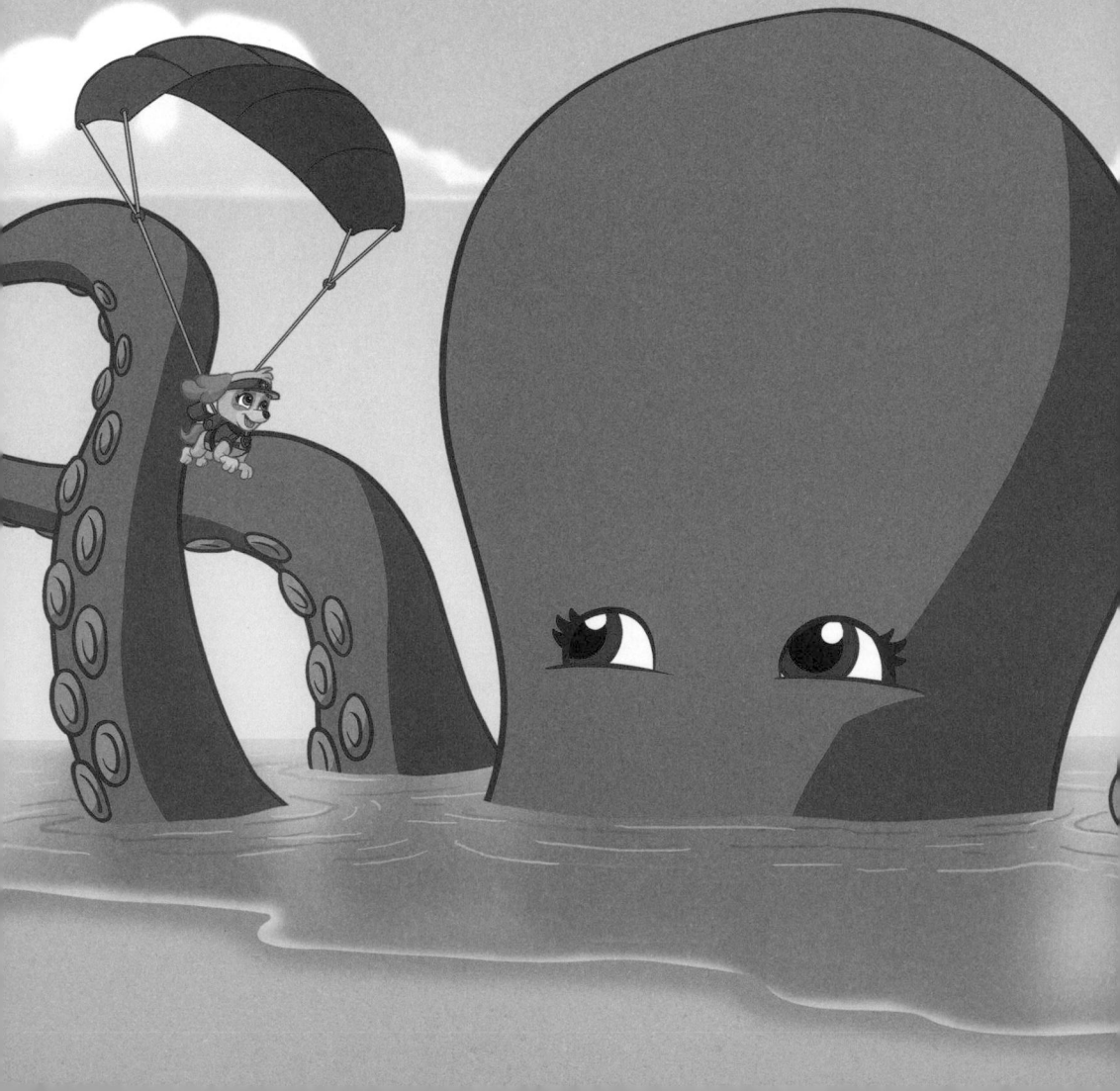

The octopus
rises out of the water.
She is looking
for her baby!

Back on the beach,
the baby octopus
jumps onto
the mayor's head!

Marshall swims
under the waves.
He finds
a baby rattle.

Marshall puts on scuba gear.

He dives into the water.

He pumps air into the boat.

The boat lifts!

Rubble uses his crane.
He lifts Cap'n Turbot
out of the water.
The baby octopus
is stuck to
the captain's life ring.

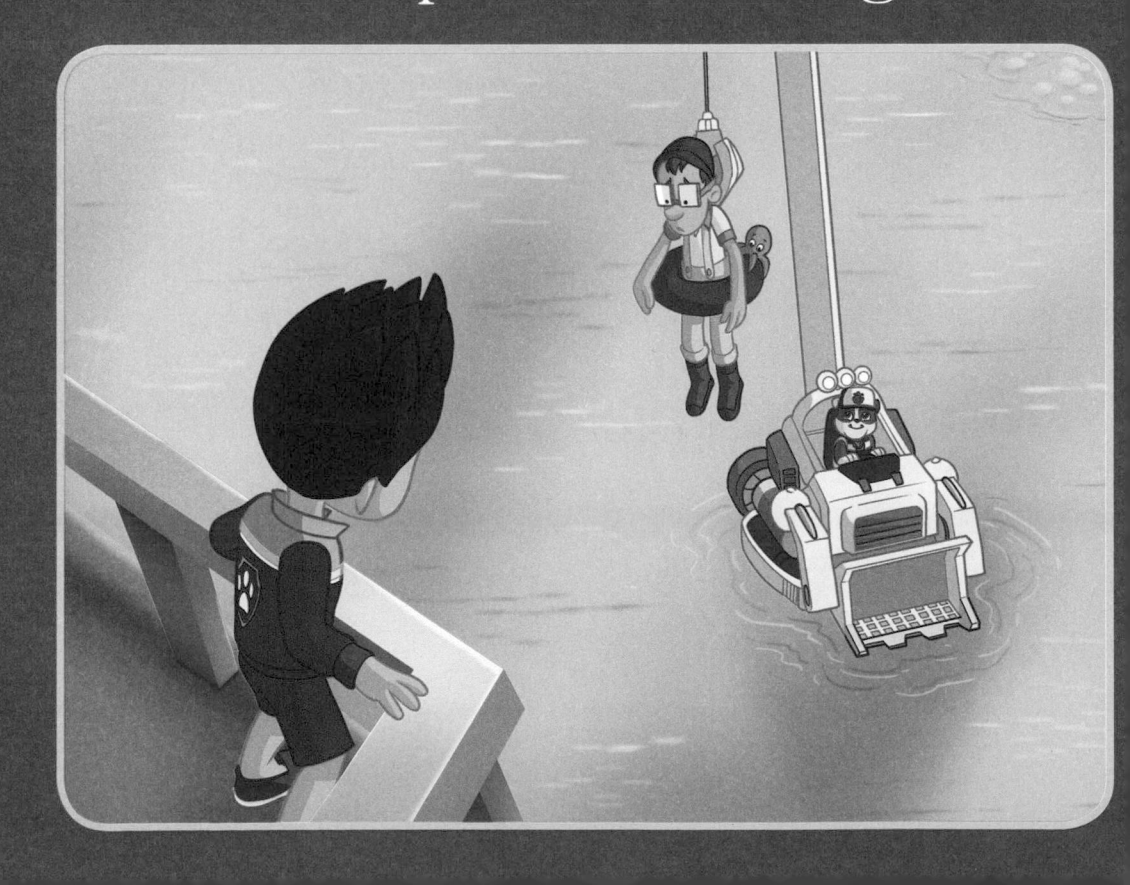

Ryder blows
the PAW Patroller's horn.
The octopus
is surprised.
It lets go of the boat.
But the boat begins to sink!

Zuma tries
to free the boat.
The big octopus
is too strong!

Robo Dog steers
the PAW Patroller
to Cap'n Turbot's boat.

The Sea Patrol is on a roll!
The pups hop aboard a ship.
Ryder tells Robo Dog
where to go.

Cap'n Turbot needs help.

He calls Ryder.

Suddenly,

an octopus appears!

It grabs the boat.

Cap'n Turbot is
out on his boat.
He does not see
a baby octopus
stuck to his bucket.

Rocky does not like
to get wet.
He will not swim!

The PAW Patrol is
also the Sea Patrol!
They are ready
to protect the beach.

STEP INTO READING®

STEP 2
READING WITH HELP

nickelodeon

PAW PATROL™

# Under the Waves!

based on the teleplay "Pups Save a Baby Octopus" by James Backshall and Jeff Sweeney

illustrated by Nate Lovett

Random House 🏠 New York

© 2018 Spin Master PAW Productions Inc. All rights reserved. Published in the United States by Random House Children's Books, a division of Penguin Random House LLC, 1745 Broadway, New York, NY 10019, and in Canada by Penguin Random House Canada Limited, Toronto. PAW Patrol and all related titles, logos, and characters are trademarks of Spin Master Ltd. Nickelodeon, Nick Jr., and all related titles and logos are trademarks of Viacom International Inc.

Step into Reading, Random House, and the Random House colophon are registered trademarks of Penguin Random House LLC.

Visit us on the Web!
StepIntoReading.com
rhcbooks.com

Educators and librarians, for a variety of teaching tools, visit us at RHTeachersLibrarians.com

ISBN 978-1-5247-7279-6 (trade) — ISBN 978-1-5247-7280-2 (lib. bdg.)

Printed in the United States of America

10 9 8 7 6 5 4 3

Random House Children's Books supports the First Amendment and celebrates the right to read.

# Dear Parents:

Congratulations! Your child is taking the first steps on an exciting journey. The destination? Independent reading!

**STEP INTO READING®** will help your child get there. The program offers five steps to reading success. Each step includes fun stories and colorful art or photographs. In addition to original fiction and books with favorite characters, there are Step into Reading Non-Fiction Readers, Phonics Readers and Boxed Sets, Sticker Readers, and Comic Readers—a complete literacy program with something to interest every child.

## Learning to Read, Step by Step!

**Ready to Read   Preschool–Kindergarten**
• big type and easy words • rhyme and rhythm • picture clues
For children who know the alphabet and are eager to begin reading.

**Reading with Help   Preschool–Grade 1**
• basic vocabulary • short sentences • simple stories
For children who recognize familiar words and sound out new words with help.

**Reading on Your Own   Grades 1–3**
• engaging characters • easy-to-follow plots • popular topics
For children who are ready to read on their own.

**Reading Paragraphs   Grades 2–3**
• challenging vocabulary • short paragraphs • exciting stories
For newly independent readers who read simple sentences with confidence.

**Ready for Chapters   Grades 2–4**
• chapters • longer paragraphs • full-color art
For children who want to take the plunge into chapter books but still like colorful pictures.

**STEP INTO READING®** is designed to give every child a successful reading experience. The grade levels are only guides; children will progress through the steps at their own speed, developing confidence in their reading.

Remember, a lifetime love of reading starts with a single step!